The Incredible Journey

Sheila Burnford

TEACHER GUIDE

NOTE:

The trade book edition of the novel used to prepare this guide is found in the Novel Units catalog and on the Novel Units website. Using other editions may have varied page references.

Please note: We have assigned Interest Levels based on our knowledge of the themes and ideas of the books included in the Novel Units sets, however, please assess the appropriateness of this novel or trade book for the age level and maturity of your students prior to reading with them. You know your students best!

ISBN 978-1-56137-468-7

Copyright infringement is a violation of Federal Law.

© 2020 by Novel Units, Inc., St. Louis, MO. All rights reserved. No part of this publication may be reproduced, translated, stored in a retrieval system, or transmitted in any way or by any means (electronic, mechanical, photocopying, recording, or otherwise) without prior written permission from Novel Units, Inc.

Reproduction of any part of this publication for an entire school or for a school system, by for-profit institutions and tutoring centers, or for commercial sale is strictly prohibited.

Novel Units is a registered trademark of Conn Education.

Printed in the United States of America.

To order, contact your local school supply store, or:

Toll-Free Fax: 877.716.7272
Phone: 888.650.4224
3901 Union Blvd., Suite 155
St. Louis, MO 63115

sales@novelunits.com

novelunits.com

Table of Contents

Novel Units: Rationale 3

Summary 5

About the Author 7

Initiating Activities..7

Discussion Questions, Vocabulary, Writing Suggestions, Activities
    Chapter One 9
    Chapter Two 13
    Chapter Three 14
    Chapter Four 15
    Chapter Five 16
    Chapter Six 17
    Chapter Seven 18
    Chapter Eight 19
    Chapter Nine..20
    Chapter Ten 21
    Chapter Eleven 22

Post-reading Discussion Questions and Activities 23

Cooperative Groups as a Strategy with the Novel Units Approach 28

Evaluations 33

Novel Units: Rationale

How do you ensure that the needs of individual students are met in a heterogeneous classroom? How do you challenge students of all abilities without losing some to confusion and others to boredom?

With the push toward "untracking" our schools, these are questions that more and more educators need to examine. As any teacher of "gifted" or "remedial" students can attest, even "homogeneous" classrooms contain students with a range of abilities and interests.

Here are some of the strategies research suggests:

- cooperative learning
- differentiated assignments
- questioning strategies that tap several levels of thinking
- flexible grouping within the class
- cross-curriculum integration
- process writing
- portfolio evaluation

Novel Units are designed with these seven facets in mind. Discussion questions and projects are framed to span all of the levels of Bloom's Taxonomy. Graphic organizers are provided to enhance critical thinking. Tests have been developed at two levels of difficulty. While most activities can be completed individually, many are ideal vehicles for collaborative effort. Throughout the guides, there is an emphasis on collaboration: students helping other students to generate ideas, students working together to actualize those ideas, and students sharing their products with other students. Extension activities link literature with other areas of the curriculum—including writing, art, music, science, history, geography, and current events—and provide a basis for portfolio evaluation.

Finally, teachers are encouraged to adapt the guides to meet the needs of individual classes and students. You know your students best! We are offering you some tools for working with them. Here are some of the "nuts and bolts" for using these "tools": a glossary of some of the terms used above that will facilitate your use of the guides.

Bloom's Taxonomy: a classification system for various levels of thinking. Questions keyed to these levels may be:

- comprehension questions, which ask one to state the meaning of what is written
- application questions, which ask one to extend one's understanding to a new situation
- analysis questions, which ask one to think about relationships between ideas such as cause/effect

- evaluation questions, which ask one to judge the accuracy of ideas
- synthesis questions, which ask one to develop a product by integrating the ideas in the text with ideas of one's own.

Graphic Organizers: visual representations of how ideas are related to each other. These "pictures"—including Venn diagrams, flow charts, attribute webs, etc.—help students collect information, make interpretations, solve problems, devise plans, and become aware of how they think.

Cooperative Learning: learning activities in which groups of two or more students collaborate. There is compelling research evidence that integration of social activities into the learning process—such as small-group discussion, group editing, group art projects—often leads to richer, more long-lasting learning.

Evaluation Portfolio: literally, a portable case for carrying loose papers and prints. More and more teachers at all levels are utilizing portfolios in assessment of student learning. See page 34 for more about the portfolio approach.

Process Writing: a way of teaching writing in which the emphasis is no longer on the product alone. Rather, students work continuously through the steps of prewriting, drafting, and revision—often through collaborative effort—in order to develop a piece for sharing with a real audience.

Summary

This is a sentimental account of how three pets—a Siamese cat, a young Labrador Retriever and an old Bull Terrier—overcome incredible hardships while journeying 250 miles across the wilderness of northern Ontario back to their owners.

Eight months earlier, the Hunter family (to whom Tao, Luath, and Bodger belong) had gone to England, where Mr. Hunter had been invited to deliver a series of lectures. Mr. Hunter's friend, John Longridge a 40-year-old bachelor and writer, had offered to let the animals stay with him until the family returned, and the Hunters had driven the 250 miles or so to John's house with the pets. The story opens in September, a few weeks before the Hunters are due back. John is preparing to take his customary hunting trip to the lakeside cabin he shares with his brother and has made arrangements with the housekeeper, Mrs. Oakes, to care for the animals while he is gone.

However, some miscommunications ensue—prompted by a faulty phone connection and the accidental burning of part of John's final instructions—and when Mrs. Oakes arrives at the house to find the animals gone, she concludes that John has decided to take them with him to the cabin. Little does she know that soon after John drove off, the cat and two dogs set out on a journey of their own—back to their beloved owners. Thus, the animals are on their own for almost three weeks before anyone—the Hunters, Mrs. Oakes, or John—is any the wiser.

Led by the young dog, the trio encounters one difficulty after another. While the cat has no trouble hunting down birds and rodents, the two dogs are soon famished—Bodger because he is too old to catch much, and the young dog because he has been trained to retrieve, not to kill. On the second day, Bodger—weak from exhaustion and hunger—is harassed and scratched by a bear cub. Luckily for Bodger, the cat and young dog come to his aid. After the cub and its mother are chased away, the cat brings a dead bird for Bodger to eat and the young dog licks Bodger's wounds.

On the third day the animals come upon some members of the Ojibway tribe cooking over a campfire. Old Bodger comes forward and is rewarded with bits of meat, the opportunity to frolic with some of the children, and attention to his wounds by one of the women. The cat ventures out to share the meat with the old white dog, then both respond to the distant summons of the young dog's barking, leaving the delighted Ojibway with the conviction that they have just hosted the legendary White Dog of Omen.

After leaving the Native American encampment, the animals cover about 15 miles a day for several days without seeing any more human beings. Then one day, while Bodger is foraging through trash cans in a lumber camp, they are terrified by the stinging blast of pellets from a shotgun. A few days later, an old man comes through the bush and the three animals follow him back to his cabin, where he chats with them as if they were human guests, ladles out four dishes of stew and proceeds to eat all of the stew himself! The next day, while the animals are fording a river, the cat is knocked unconscious by debris from a beaver dam and swept downstream, where a little Finnish girl, Helvi, finds him. Helvi's father revives the cat and over the next few days Helvi grows closer and closer to her new pet; then on the fourth night, Helvi watches tearfully as Tao heads off into the moonlight to find his friends.

Meanwhile, the young dog has gotten into a fight with a collie after killing a chicken from the collie's farm. Bodger comes to the young dog's aid, and both scamper off just as the farmer appears. Next, the Lab has an encounter with a porcupine that leaves quills deeply and painfully embedded in his muzzle.

On his own now, the cat is attacked by a lynx, who would probably have gotten the better of the Siamese if not for the boy who came along with a deer-hunting rifle and killed the lynx. Two days later, Tao reunites with the dogs. A forester sights the threesome, but cannot get anyone to believe that he has seen three household pets in the wild. The animals come to a hamlet, where they are chased away, then to a farm, where a kindly old couple—the Mackenzies—feed them and remove the quills from the Labrador.

John Longridge returns home and is horrified to discover the animals' absence and presumes the death of at least the old dog and the small cat. Shortly thereafter, the Hunters return from England and receive the sad news that their pets are gone. Hoping that at least Luath might have survived in the wilderness, John Longridge searches for witnesses who may have seen the animals and is inundated with phone calls. For a week, he and the Hunters try to track down the animals' whereabouts through the phone calls. Then, weary and discouraged, John suggests that they all go to the Hunters' summer cottage—which lies along the western route the animals would have taken—to celebrate Peter's 12th birthday.

On the last afternoon there, the unbelievable happens. While out on a walk, John and the Hunters are delighted to hear the barking of Luath, whose appearance is followed by that of Tao and, after several minutes that are almost heart-breaking to Peter, who has grown up with the old dog, by the appearance of Bodger.

About the Author

Sheila Burnford was born in Scotland on May 11, 1918. She went to St. George's School in Edinburgh and Harrogate College in Yorkshire before studying in Germany. After marrying David Burnford in 1941, she had three daughters. She served in the Royal Naval Hospital's Voluntary Aid Detachment in England between 1939 and 1941, and served as an ambulance driver the following year. She died in 1984, at age 65.

The Incredible Journey was one of two books Burnford wrote for children, and by far the more popular. She wrote two other novels, *The Fields of Noon* and *Without Reserve*, and was a contributor to *Punch*, *Canadian Poetry* and *The Glasgow Herald*.

Initiating Activities

Choose one or more of the following activities to establish an appropriate mind set for the story students are about to read:

1. **Anticipation Guide** (See Novel Units Student Packet, Activity Sheet #3): Students discuss their opinions of statements which tap themes they will meet in the story, e.g., friendship, animal behavior, survival, etc.

2. **Video:** View the video version of the novel.

3. Have students **brainstorm** associations with the word INSTINCT as a student scribe jots ideas around the word on a large piece of paper. Help students "cluster" the ideas into categories. A sample framework is shown below:

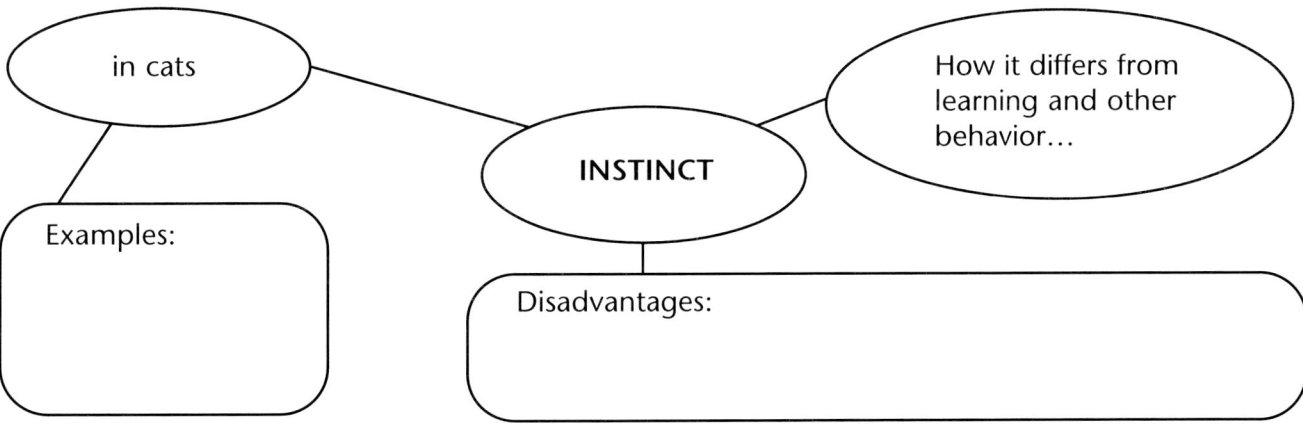

4. **Prediction:** After looking at the cover and flipping through the book, what can you tell about the story? What do you predict happens to the three animals on the cover? Why are they together? What problems will they face? Why do they take the journey? What is "incredible" about the journey?

5. **Pre-reading Discussion**
    ...of animal friendships—Do you know any animals who seem to be friends? How do they show friendship? How do they greet each other after a separation? How do they help each other?
    ...of animal wanderings—Have you ever moved to a new house with cats and/or dogs? How did they react to the new place? How did you make sure that they didn't get lost the first time they went outside? Have any of your pets ever gone on a long wander? Were they able to find their way back again? Why did they leave?
    ...of dogs and cats—What do you know about Bull Terriers? Labrador Retrievers? Siamese cats? How do they look? How do they act? What do you think determines a pet's personality? How much does the personality of the owner have to do with it? How do cats and dogs in the same household tend to get along?
    ...of survival—What basics do animals and humans need to survive? What else do you need to survive? What else do your pets need to survive happily?

6. **Pre-reading Journal Writing:**
    Free write for ten minutes, nonstop, beginning with one of the following phrases:
    - Animals can be a lot like people...
    - I know of some animals who seem to be friends with each other...
    - Losing a pet...

7. After reading each chapter, students **rate the tension of the story** on the following scale:

NOT MUCH EXCITEMENT   **VERY EXCITING**

        1   2   3   4   5   6

8. **Dialectical Journal**
    Students keep a two-column journal. They summarize the plot of each section they have read in the left hand column, and react to the reading in the right hand column. (This might include statements that begin, "That reminds me of the time my dog...," "I wonder if the cat..." "That is like the movie..." etc.)

Discussion Questions • Vocabulary
Writing Suggestions • Activities

Chapter One

Vocabulary Words

timber lanes (1)	concessions (1)	amphibious (2)	migratory flyway (2)
burnished (2)	exhilarating (2)	austerely (3)	domestic (3)
accord (3)	sapphire (4)	translucent (4)	whip-tapered (4)
prime (4)	sinew (4)	docile (4)	irrepressible (4)
forebears (5)	asters (5)	contrition (6)	amends (6)
reproof (7)	sybaritic (7)	reprieve (8)	enticed (8)
trellised (8)	indefinable (8)	assented (9)	in thrall (10)
lash (10)	reciprocal (12)	appalled (12)	prelude (12)
languished (13)	martyred (13)	incessant (13)	resign (13)

Vocabulary Activity: Word mapping is an activity that lends itself to any vocabulary list. For words that have clear antonyms, the following framework is suitable:

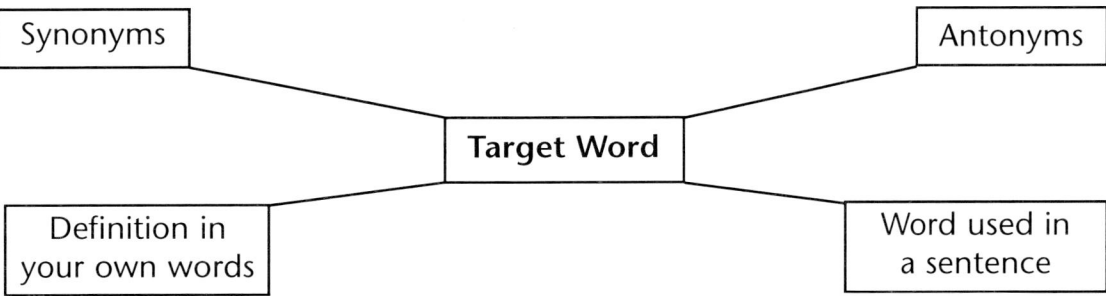

Students might enjoy coming up with variations on this framework. For example, instead of listing antonyms, students could provide line drawings to illustrate the target word.

Cooperative Learning Activity: Each individual within a small group is responsible for three or four words. Each group member teaches the others about these words by sharing his/her maps with the others. Students are tested individually on all the words, but all members of a group get bonus points if everyone gets above a certain score.

Discussion Questions

1. Where is the story set? When? Is this a place and time in which you would have liked to live? *(wilderness of northwestern Ontario, Canada, probably late 1950's or early 1960's)*

2. Who is shown in the picture next to page 1? How have these three animals come to be with the man? How do they all seem to feel about each other? *(John Longridge, Tao-cat, Bodger-old Bull Terrier and Luath-young Labrador; John, a writer, has offered to let the animals stay with him for nine months while their owners, the Hunters, go to England where Jim Hunter has been asked to deliver some lectures; the animals are friends and miss their owners, but are getting used to John, who is getting attached to them.)*

3. What are your impressions of the Terrier, the Labrador, and the Siamese? (Begin an Attribute Web for each, see the following page.) How do they differ in temperament? Do they remind you of any pets you have had or known? *(The old Terrier is sly, lazy, merry, likes children; the young Lab is serious, enjoys hunting with his adored master; the Siamese is aloof, skilled at opening doors, independent.)*

4. What effect does the man's attention to his gun have on the young dog? Why? Why does the man replace the gun "in sudden contrition"? (p. 6) *(The man is checking his gun in preparation for the trip he will take, and the dog, who loves to retrieve ducks, pricks up his ears in interest; the man is apologetic because he gave the dog false hopes.)*

5. Why does Mrs. Oakes call John? Why does John write her a note? *(John and his housekeeper want to firm up plans for what is to be done while he is visiting his brother; when the phone goes dead, John writes a note to tell Mrs. Oakes that he needs her to order some food and that he has already fed the dogs.)*

6. Why does John scold the old dog? What effect does the scolding have? *(The dog sneaks up onto the chair while John is on the phone; the dog acts mournful and John laughs.)*

7. Where is John planning to go? What will he do with the animals? What other choices does he have? What do you do with your pets when you go away? *(Twice a year, he and his brother get together to fish or hunt at a cabin 200 miles away; he could board the animals, but Mrs. Oakes offers to watch them.)*

8. How far are the animals from their original home? How many times have they made the trip by car? When are their owners planning to come for them? *(250 miles; the Hunters drove them to John's house once, eight months ago and are coming back for them in a couple of weeks.)*

9. Each of the animals "belongs" to one of the Hunters. Explain which animal is closest to which person and why. What sort of "last-minute instructions" (p.13) do you suppose Peter left with John concerning the pets? *(Elizabeth feeds and brushes the cat and he sleeps at the foot of her bed; Peter has been inseparable from the terrier since the puppy arrived on Peter's first birthday; the Labrador belongs to the father, who trained him since puppyhood.)*

10. What happens to one page of John's note to Mrs. Oakes? What did that page say? *(When the cat knocks over the paperweight, one page flutters into the fireplace and burns. The first page ends "I will be taking the dogs (and Tao too, of course!)..." The lost page continues "...out for a run before I leave.")*

Prediction: One page of John's note has burned. What will be the result?

Writing Activity: You are Jim Hunter. Drop John a postcard from England. Tell how you and the children are doing, and don't forget to mention your pets. (The "postcard" might be a small piece of poster board with a picture of a British landmark drawn or pasted on one side.)

Using Character Webs in the Novel Unit Approach

Attribute webs are simply a visual representation of a character from the novel. They provide a systematic way for students to organize and recap the information they have about a particular character. Attribute webs may be used after reading the novel to recapitulate information about a particular character, or completed gradually as information unfolds. They may be completed individually or as a group project.

One type of character attribute web uses these divisions:

- How a character acts and feels. (How does the character act? How do you think the character feels? How would you feel if this happened to you?)

- How a character looks. (Close your eyes and picture the character. Describe him/her to me.)

- Where a character lives. (Where and when does the character live?)

- How others feel about the character. (How does another specific character feel about our character?)

In group discussion about the characters described in student attribute webs, the teacher can ask for backup proof from the novel. Inferential thinking can be included in the discussion.

Attribute webs need not be confined to characters. They may also be used to organize information about a concept, object, or place.

Attribute Web

The attribute web below will help you gather clues the author provides about a character in the novel. Fill in the blanks with words and phrases which tell how the character acts and looks, as well as what the character says and what others say about him or her.

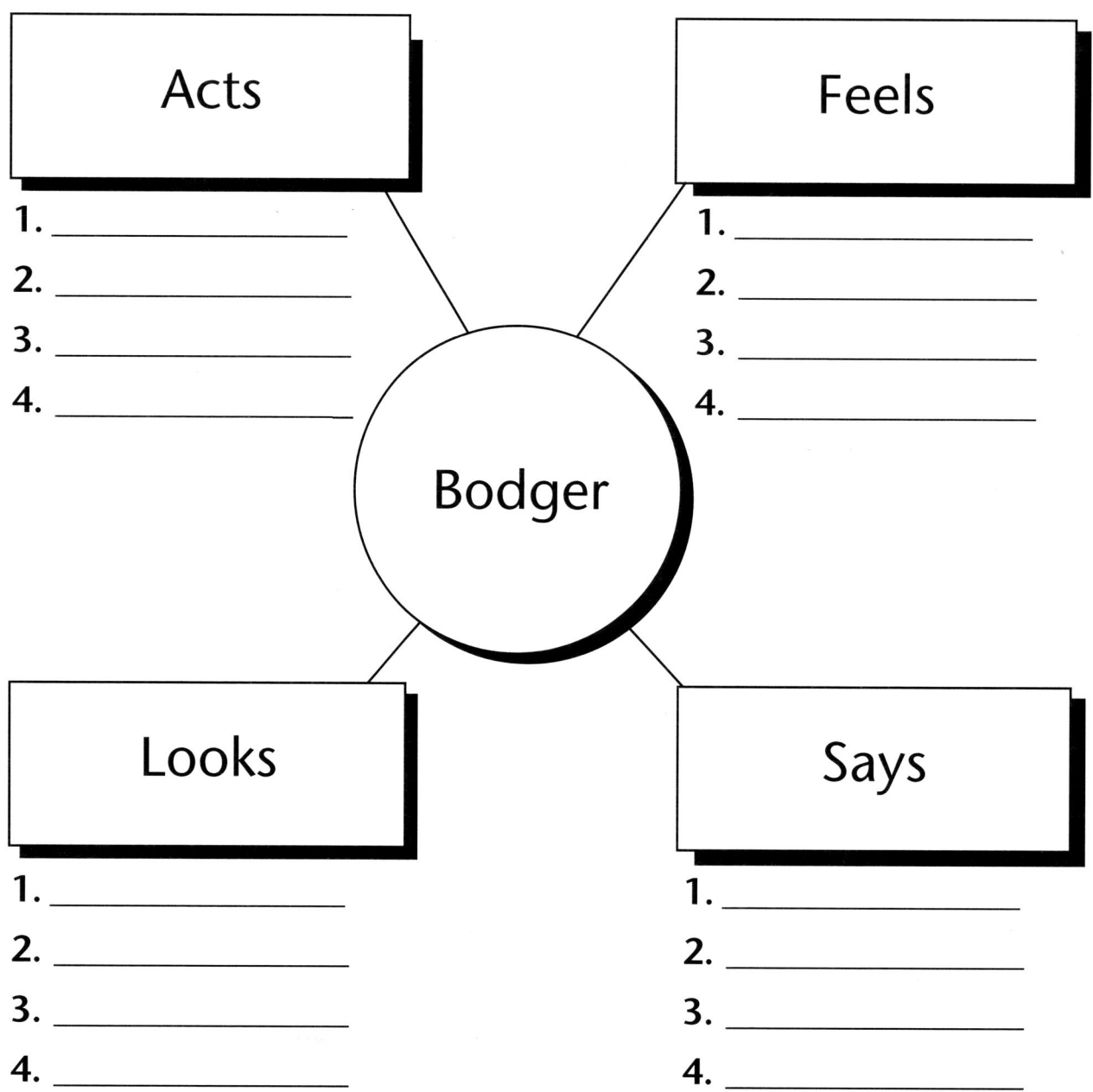

Acts
1. _____
2. _____
3. _____
4. _____

Feels
1. _____
2. _____
3. _____
4. _____

Bodger

Looks
1. _____
2. _____
3. _____
4. _____

Says
1. _____
2. _____
3. _____
4. _____

Chapter Two

Vocabulary Words

adjacent (18) methodically (18) wistfully (19) materialize (20)
placid (20) wary (24)

Discussion Questions

1. Why does John almost wish he didn't have to leave Luath just now? (*Luath has finally shown him some trust and affection by offering him a paw.*)

2. Why does John feel a little silly about his farewell to the animals? Do you agree with him that he is "becoming too attached to them"? (*He waves to them from his car.*)

3. How would John feel if he could see what happens to the animals twenty minutes after he leaves? (*He would be shocked to see them head off down the road; they never wander far from the house.*)

4. Who leads the group? How do they decide which way to go? Are they going in the proper direction? (*Luath, the young Labrador leads, heading instinctively west which is the direction from which the Hunters brought them.*)

5. Why does Mrs. Oakes think that something is odd when she arrives? Why does she stop worrying? (*She doesn't see the animals, but is reassured when she reads the part of the note which is left because it seems to indicate that John has decided to take the pets with him.*)

6. How do you imagine the scene when darkness falls the first night of the trip? Where do the three sleep? What sounds do you hear? What do you smell? What is the temperature like? (*The old dog is asleep; the young dog and cat come to sleep nearby; we hear the wolf, owls, rustling, porcupine; the temperature is probably crisp but not bitterly cold.*)

Prediction: Already Bodger is exhausted. Besides fatigue, what problems will the animals face?

Writing Activity: On pages 20-22, we see Mrs. Oakes' reaction when she finds that the animals are gone, presumably with John. Rewrite this section, telling how Mrs. Oakes would have acted if all pages of the note had been clipped together, and she had known that the animals were supposed to be at home.

Chapter Three

Vocabulary Words

gullet (29)	appease (30)	sedge (31)	abhorrent (31)
plaintive (32)	unresponsive (32)	benison (32)	whisky-jack (34)
transfixed (35)	ineffectual (36)	banshee (36)	adversary (36)
decamp (37)	bravado (37)	rank (37)	stanch (37)
perplexity (38)	galvanizing (38)	grotesque (38)	harlequin (38)
succulent (39)			

Discussion Questions

1. What can you figure out about the cat's actions before the others wake up? *(He goes out to hunt and finds a bird.)*

2. How can you tell that the young dog considers the old dog's needs when choosing particular routes? *(He chooses the softer, more shaded areas because "these were all considerations that the old dog needed.")*

3. Why does the cat do better than the dogs when it comes to getting food? Why do you think the Terrier isn't a better hunter? What about the Labrador? What advice would you give these dogs about how to get food? *(The cat's hunting instincts have not been trained out of him. The Terrier is old, has poor eyesight, and is pretty slow; the Labrador has been trained not to eat the animals it retrieves.)*

4. Why does Bodger collapse? *(He is old, weary, hungry.)*

5. What happens before and after what is shown in the picture on page 28? *(A cub bats at Bodger and the cat attacks the cub; the mother bear comes to investigate, and Luath and Tao manage to scare her and the cub away.)*

6. What do you think would have happened to Bodger if the mother bear hadn't come along? if the cat hadn't come along? if the Labrador hadn't come along? *(If the cat hadn't upset the mother by attacking her cub, perhaps the bears would have left Bodger alone; however, once the cat attacked the cub, Bodger would have been a goner without the intervention of the dog.)*

7. How do the cat and the Labrador help their friend, Bodger, recover after his encounter with the bears? Do you think these are actions a cat and dog would really take? *(The cat brings Bodger food and the young dog licks Bodger's wounds.)*

Prediction: A bear and her cub have been driven away. What other wild animals might attack the trio?

Writing Activity: You are Bodger. If you could write, what "thank you" poem might you give to Luath, the Labrador?

Chapter Four

Vocabulary Words

forage (41)	pulsating (42)	ambling (42)	silhouetted (43)
immersion (43)	cantering (43)	tantalizing (44)	compound (44)
chaff (45)	crestfallen (46)	paroxysms (46)	derision (47)
skirted (48)	imperatively (48)	resignedly (48)	impassively (48)
succored (49)			

Discussion Questions

1. What does the Labrador try eating at first? What does it mean that "the generations fell away" (p. 42) when he finally killed and ate a rabbit? *(berries, deer droppings; He finally overcame the genetically-reinforced aversion to eating dead animals—an aversion that has been instilled in Labradors for generations by their hunter-owners.)*

2. What leads the animals to the Ojibway campsite? *(They smell food cooking.)*

3. How do the Ojibway treat the old dog? *(At first one child is frightened, but the adults pet and feed him and the other children play with him.)*

4. Why do the Ojibway laugh at the cat? *(He takes food away from Bodger.)*

5. How does the Ojibway woman treat the old dog's wounds? *(She places wet moss on the cuts.)*

6. How can you tell that the young dog is more cautious about humans than the other two animals are? *(He stays hidden.)*

7. Why don't the Terrier and cat stay with the Ojibway longer? *(They hear the young Labrador call to them.)*

8. What is the meaning of the statement on page 49: "That night they became immortal"? *(The Ojibway decide that these mortal animals are actually legendary spirits.)*

Prediction: Based on the picture you see on page 50, what danger do you think the animals face in the next chapter? Which animal is in the most danger?

Writing Activity: Do some research on the Ojibways (also called Chippewas) and write a brief report. Include details about geographical location, language, food, shelter, economy, culture.

Chapter Five

Vocabulary Words

stolid (52)	lodestone (52)	nomadic (53)	debonair (53)
compensate (53)	flourished (54)	complacent (54)	buntings (54)
exultant (54)	tempo (55)	marauding (55)	ford (56)
bracken (56)	pottered (56)	connoisseur (57)	procession (57)
deference (59)	irresolute (59)	fastidiously (59)	nonplussed (60)
diffusing (60)	cavalier (63)	transports (63)	mariner (63)
pent-up (64)	debris (65)	impetus (65)	foothold (65)
flanks (66)	requiem (66)		

Discussion Questions

1. How does the nomadic life seem to agree with the three animals? How are their "attitudes" different? Which has a "personality" most like yours? *(Positive, good-humored Bodger becomes healthier; the resourceful cat maintains his health; the gentle, worried Labrador grows very thin and is often hungry.)*

2. In what sort of place do the animals like to sleep? Why? *(They look for areas under uprooted trees where they can stay dry and be protected from the wind.)*

3. What are some signs of the changing season? How do these changes affect the trio? *(Leaves are falling off the trees; it is getting colder at night; rabbits are changing their coats to winter white; animals are preparing for hibernation. The cold is hard on the animals.)*

4. Why does someone shoot at the animals? *(Bodger is foraging through trash cans outside a lumber camp.)*

5. How does the old recluse treat the animals? Why? Do they trust him? *(He treats them like human guests, politely showing them into his house; they seem to trust him, although Luath isn't quite sure about the whole thing.)*

6. Why don't the animals enjoy the stew? *(The man eats what is in all the dishes, thinking that if the animals aren't eating, they must not be hungry.)*

7. Why doesn't the cat try to catch the chipmunk inside the old man's cabin? *(He seems to sense that it would be wrong to kill his host's pet.)*

8. Why does the young dog decide to enter the river? What other choices does he have? *(He could keep following alongside it, looking for a place to ford, but he is frustrated about going in the wrong direction and the river seems to be growing wider, not narrower.)*

9. What problem arises when the animals enter the river? Explain what is shown in the picture. *(The cat is swept downstream and the debris from a beaver dam knocks him unconscious.)*

10. How do the dogs respond to the loss of their friend, the cat? Is this detail a contradiction of Whitman's statement about "beasts" that "They do not sweat and whine about their condition/They do not lie awake in the dark and weep for their sins...Not one is dissatisfied..." *(They try to help him, then give up and grieve; the old dog howls in the night.)*

Prediction: What will happen to the cat? Will he be reunited with the dogs?

Writing Activity: The old dog "howled his requiem of grief" upon losing his friend, the cat. Describe a time when you experienced grief. How did you express it?

Chapter Six

Vocabulary Words

uncompromising (69)	frugal (69)	wrested (70)	subjection (70)
heralded (70)	eddy (70)	bedraggled (71)	disheveled (72)
spasm (72)	convulsively (72)	pulsate (72)	throaty (73)
incongruous (74)	vantage (75)	harrow (75)	companionship (75)
austerity (76)	vigilance (76)	simian (76)	illustrious (77)
zealous (77)	regal (77)	pungent (78)	enigma (78)
sinuous (78)	desolate (78)	wraith (79)	

Discussion Questions

1. What sort of life do the Nurmis lead? Would you be satisfied with that sort of life? *(They live alone; they live frugally, surviving off the land—farming, trapping.)*

2. How does Helvi end up with the cat? Why hasn't she had pets before? *(She finds the wet cat while she is skipping stones; the family has been too poor to feed a pet that does not earn its keep.)*

3. How do the Nurmis try to revive the cat? What do you think a veterinarian would do? *(rubbing it dry, pouring warm milk and brandy down its throat, pressing the water out of its lungs, putting him in a warm oven)*

4. How can you tell that the cat has been missing human companionship? *(He follows the Nurmis around.)*

5. What is a "traveling library"? What sort of books does Helvi take out? What books would you recommend to her? Do you think she would enjoy this novel? *(Rural areas and small towns not big enough to support a permanent library often have vans/trucks that drive around with books; Helvi takes out all sorts of books about Siamese cats.)*

6. How long does the cat stay with the Nurmis? Why does he leave? *(After four days, he regains his hearing.)*

7. How can you tell that the cat can hear now? *(He orients toward Helvi's voice.)*

8. How does Helvi feel as she watches the cat go? How would you feel? Do you think she would rather that he had left while she slept? *(She is sad, but realizes that it is time for him to go, that her usefulness to the cat is over.)*

Prediction: Will Helvi ever see the cat again? Where will the cat go now?

Writing Activities: (1) You are Helvi. Write an entry in your journal the night after the cat leaves. Describe how she came into your life, how you spent your time together, and how you feel now that she is gone. Or (2) Research Siamese cats and write a brief report.

Chapter Seven

Vocabulary Words

apparition (81)	avowed (81)	feline (81)	capitulated (81)
sallied (82)	homage (82)	dispatching (82)	fisher (82)
bittern (82)	voraciously (83)	compact (84)	projectile (84)
slewed (84)	onslaughts (85)	whirling dervish (85)	unprecedented (85)
incredulously (85)	unscathed (85)	insolence (86)	morale (86)
infectiously (86)	foraging (87)	delectable (87)	

Discussion Questions

1. How did the Terrier and cat get along at first? Why do they have a "special" relationship now? *(The dog didn't like cats, and the kitten was prepared to fight, but they soon became fast friends—driving off other cats and dogs.)*

2. How does the Labrador get into a fight with a collie? What do you think would have happened if Bodger hadn't joined in? *(The collie catches the Lab and Terrier eating one of his master's chickens and the collie attacks; the young dog is losing the fight until the Terrier, an instinctive fighter, joins the fray.)*

3. How does the old dog's attitude change after the fight with the collie? *(His morale is restored.)*

4. Why does the Lab attack the porcupine? What is the result? *(He remembers the meal of porcupine provided by the fisher; he gets a lot of quills in his muzzle.)*

5. Why didn't the fisher end up injured by the porcupine it had caught earlier? *(The fisher had skillfully flipped the porcupine after teasing it into shooting most of its quills into a stump. There are no quills in the underbelly.)*

6. Why can't the young dog get the quills out? *(The quills are pliable and their barbed ends only work in deeper when Luath paws at his mouth.)*

Prediction: The Lab can't get the quills out. How will these quills affect him? Who will get them out?

Writing Activity: You work for the Department of Animal Control. A farmer has called to complain about a fight between his dog and two other dogs that came onto your property. Take down the farmer's "eyewitness account" of what happened and write it in report form for your files.

Chapter Eight

Vocabulary Words

baleful (91)	venturing (91)	dislodged (92)	scrutiny (92)
marten (92)	disdain (92)	excreta (92)	decoy (93)
poseur (94)	overlaid (95)	wanton (95)	remorseless (96)
lynx (95)	malevolent (97)	pistons (97)	tawny (97)
assured (100)	intricate (100)	alight (101)	expressive (101)

Discussion Questions

1. What instinctive behaviors are in evidence as the cat proceeds on his way? *(He moves quietly, covers all traces of food eaten, tracks, excreta, etc., sleeps high in a tree.)*

2. How long does it take the cat to locate his friends? How does the weather slow him? *(It takes him two days; because of the rain, he stops to take cover often.)*

3. Who calls "Here kitty, kitty"? Why do you suppose the cat doesn't respond? *(Hunters; perhaps the cat doesn't trust them.)*

4. Who follows the cat? *(a lynx)* Why do you think the narrator refers to that animal as "something evil" and "remorseless"? Do you agree that the predator is "evil"?

5. What strategies does the lynx use to try to get the cat? *(He tries to follow the cat up the tree, tries to shake the cat off a second tree, digs at the rabbit burrow where the cat hides.)*

6. What do you think would have happened if the boy hadn't come along or if his aim had not been accurate? *(The lynx probably would have killed the cat; a lynx would probably run if someone shot at it and missed.)*

7. How do the three animals behave when the cat finds his friends? *(The old dog runs happy circles around the cat, who climbs a tree and jumps on Bodger's back; then the Lab walks up to the cat, who puts his forepaws on the Lab's neck.)*

Prediction: How long will it be before everyone finds out that the animals are missing? How will John and the Hunter family react?

Writing Activity: Write the conversation the boy has with his mother when he returns home after hunting with his father.

Chapter Nine

Vocabulary Words

unscathed (103)	access (103)	carcass (103)	hue and cry (104)
sublimely (105)	resolutely (105)	primeval (105)	habitation (106)
porcine (106)	brandishing (107)	overtures (108)	smokehouse (108)
cornucopias (109)	artillery (109)	leer (109)	tempo (109)
gargoyle (109)	proffered (109)	succession (110)	pretexts (110)
distended (111)	indefatigable (112)	unavailingly (112)	mallards (112)
recumbent (113)	infinitesimal (113)	tableau (114)	travesty (116)
emboldened (119)	beyond the pale (119)	skirmishes (119)	boisterous (119)
incisor (120)	indignantly (121)	replete (122)	laggard (123)

Discussion Questions

1. How many miles have the animals covered? How far do you figure they have to go? *(200 miles covered, 50 to go)*

2. Who sees the animals? Explain what you think is meant by the statement that "the forester was able to return the laugh a week later." (p.104) *(A timber-cruising forester sees them, but the senior forester laughs at the idea that household pets are tramping around the wilderness; presumably the senior forester stops laughing and believes the other forester when he hears from the pets' owners.)*

3. Why does the young dog decide to lead the other two animals toward human habitation? *(He fears the wolf that has been following them.)*

4. Why is the old dog so surprised to have the bucket of water thrown in his face? Hasn't he ever seen human anger before? *(He has been the object of anger before, but never for no reason.)*

5. Why does the Terrier approach the Mackenzies? How is their reaction different from that of the man who turned the dog away the day before? *(The Terrier smells the bacon; the old couple welcome him and feed him.)*

6. Why does the Lab, who stayed away when the other two approached the Ojibway, decide to approach Mr. Mackenzie? *(He retrieves instinctively when Mr. Mackenzie shoots the bird.)*

7. What is the Lab's main physical problem? How does Mr. Mackenzie treat that problem? Do you find the Lab's response during the treatment believable? *(Mr. Mackenzie pulls out the porcupine quills; the dog is quiet and grateful, trying to lick his hand in thanks.)*

8. How do the Mackenzies deduce that the old dog and the young one are from the same family? *(They act familiar with each other; Bodger tries to get in to "defend" Luath when the Mackenzies shut him out so they can tend Luath's wounds.)*

9. The Mackenzies hear a cat fight. What do you think that is all about? What is surprising about the way the two dogs react to the noise? *(The two dogs seem pleased by the noise; Tao is probably fighting with the farm cats.)*

10. How do the dogs get out of the latched stable as they begin the last leg of their journey? *(The cat opens the latch.)* How do you think the old couple reacted when they discovered the animals missing?

Prediction: Will the animals survive the last 50 miles? What new dangers will this rugged country present?

Writing Activity: You are Nell. Write a letter to one of your grown children about the two dogs that have been visiting with you and your husband.

Group Activity: As a whole class, use an extended T-diagram to compare the different experiences of the three animals while they were at the Mackenzie's.

Tao	Bodger	Luath
never seen by humans	made the decision to go to the farm	arrived by accident, following his instinct to retrieve a duck
no elaborate meals	enjoyed gorging on food	ate ravenously
had fights with farm cats	adored by all, as he expected	finally must depend on human help

Chapter Ten

Vocabulary Words

panorama (127)	reassured (128)	bleak (128)	unresponsive (128)
charges (129)	befallen (129)	disparate (129)	oppressive (130)
forlorn (131)	inconsolable (131)	ominous (132)	circulated (132)
bush pilot (132)	clearinghouse (133)	despondent (133)	dejectedly (134)
diffidently (134)	recluse (135)		

Discussion Questions

1. What route are the Hunters taking home? What do you think they are thinking/saying as they approach Montreal? *(They are on the final stretch up the St. Lawrence via ferry; they are probably chattering about seeing their pets again; Elizabeth has gotten a red collar for the cat; Peter is looking forward to seeing Bodger; their father is eagerly anticipating hunting with Luath.)*

2. How do you think John discovered what had happened to the animals? What do you think he and Mrs. Oakes said to each other? *(John returned home from his trip, found the animals gone, contacted Mrs. Oakes who—horrified—explained that she assumed the animals were with John.)*

3. Does John still hope that the animals are alive? Why or why not? *(He holds out scant hope, and only that for the young dog, because of the harshness of the environment and the threat of wild animals, traps, poison, and other dangers.)*

4. What steps does John take to trace the animals? Can you think of additional people you would call? *(He calls the Chief Ranger of Lands and Forests who circulates word to the game wardens and foresters; he also tries calling a bush pilot, a newspaper editor, the superintendent of a hydro maintenance crew, a rural phone supervisor.)*

5. Who reports having seen the animals? *(Helvi, someone who talked with the addled old man.)*

6. Why does John discount the information about the old recluse? Is he correct to do so? *(He assumes that the man was just imagining that he had guests, since he mentioned no animals.)*

Prediction: Will the Hunter family be reunited with their pets? If so, how and where?

Writing Activity: Make a "Lost Pets" poster. Be sure to include a picture of the animals, description of identifying marks, names, where they were last seen, contact person, etc. or write the letter that John gets from his goddaughter, Elizabeth (p.128).

Chapter Eleven

Vocabulary Words

surly (138)	unrepentant (138)	undermine (138)	conviction (138)
penitent (139)	truant (139)	pored (139)	terrain (139)
disillusionment (140)	indefinable (141)	companionable (141)	savor (141)
martyrdom (142)	diligent (142)	wily (142)	poignant (142)
expectancy (143)	taut (144)	discordant (144)	gaunt (144)
inarticulate (145)	vestige (145)	raucous (145)	pandemonium (145)
rebuff (146)	prised (146)	surreptitiously (146)	nautical (147)
indistinguishable (147)			

Discussion Questions

1. Most of the sightings are of the dogs and soon nothing further is heard of the cat. Why do you think that is? *(The cat often managed to move quietly and remain unseen.)*

2. Peter and Elizabeth react very differently to the news that their pets are gone. What is the difference? *(Peter grieves quietly, without hope; Elizabeth is sure her cat is alive.)*

3. Who is the cousin that reports the spell cast over the rice crop? Who is the farmer and how does he exaggerate? *(one of the Ojibway; The farmer is the one whose collie fought the two dogs; his collie isn't peaceloving, Bodger isn't vicious and powerful, only one chicken was killed—not a prize-winning flock.)*

4. What trip does Longridge suggest to the Hunters? Why? *(To get away from the depressing phone calls/false leads and to celebrate Peter's 12th birthday, John suggests going to the Hunters' summer cottage on Lake Windigo.)*

5. Why does Elizabeth hesitate to go on the trip? Why does she decide that it is all right to go? *(She is afraid that her cat will return home to find her missing, but John convinces her that the cottage is on the route the cat would take.)*

6. Why do the summer cottage and its surroundings seem different from usual? Have you ever had an experience like this—a trip to a spot you usually visit only in the summer? *(The Hunters are used to being there during the summer; many of the other cottages are shuttered and the lake is nearly empty of boats.)*

7. How do the children spend most of their time at the cottage? *(Peter takes pictures of animals and Elizabeth plays in the treehouse.)*

8. Why does Peter remember this time last year? What happened when he tried to teach Bodger to retrieve? *(He tried to teach Bodger to retrieve, but the old dog deliberately buried the glove.)*

9. In what order do the animals return? How are they greeted? Why doesn't Peter act more affectionate toward Luath? Why does Tao streak up the trail at the end? *(The cat, an instant later—the Lab; Peter is afraid that his own beloved Bodger is not returning but several minutes later the old dog does show up; the cat wants to end the journey with his old friend.)*

Writing Activity: The author does not describe the scene where the children learn that their pets are missing. Write that scene. Explain who talks with the two children and how each reacts.

Post-reading Discussion Questions and Activities

1. Why did Burnford choose to call her novel *The Incredible Journey*? What other titles would have been good?

2. What problems did the animals have to overcome? What are some examples of the animals' instinctive behavior? At what points did the animals act like people in the way they approached their problems and each other? Did you find the story believable? Could it really happen?

3. What are some problems the animals might have had but didn't?

4. In your opinion, which picture showed the most important thing that happened in the story? How much do you think the pictures added to your enjoyment/understanding of the story?

5. How were the three animals different from each other? How were they alike?

6. How did Luath, Bodger, and Tao change during their journey? Do you think they will act any differently, now that they are back with their families once again?

7. John has grown quite close to these pets. How do you think he will cope with living alone again?

8. If you could have one of these three pets, which would you choose? Why? Did any of the three remind you of pets you have had?

9. What was your favorite part of the story? Why?

10. Do you have any questions about the story? Did you like the ending? Would you have added anything to it, if you were the writer?

11. What did you learn from the story about cats? dogs? other animals? Canada?

12. Suppose the story had been written this year about three animals who live in a U.S. city. What changes would have to be made in the story? How important is the setting to Sheila Burnford's story?

13. Do you know another story similar to this one? What is it? How is it similar? How, for example, is it similar to other survival tales you may have read?

14. What qualities of the main characters are critical for coping with conditions that threaten survival? Do you think the three animals could have survived if they hadn't helped each other?

15. How is reading this story like doing a jigsaw puzzle? What techniques does the author use to "feed" you pieces of the puzzle?

Suggested Further Reading

Other animal stories:
    Old Yeller—Fred Gipson (Novel Unit Available)
    The Animal Family—Randall Jarrell
    Big Red—Jim Kjelgaard (Novel Unit Available)
    Sounder—William Armstrong (Novel Unit Available)
    The Black Stallion (Series)—Walter Farley (Novel Unit Available)
    Owls in the Family—Farley Mowat (Novel Unit Available)
    Woodsong—Gary Paulsen (Novel Unit Available)

King of the Wind—Marguerite Henry (Novel Unit Available)
Summer of the Monkeys—Wilson Rawls (Novel Unit Available)
Where the Red Fern Grows—Wilson Rawls (Novel Unit Available)
A Time to Fly Free—Stephanie S. Tolan
Julie of the Wolves; My Side of the Mountain—Jean Craighead George (Novel Unit Available)

Drama/Oral Activity
1. Dramatize your favorite scene from the book, using finger puppets or actors.

2. Write a scene that never happens in the story but might have.

3. Assume the persona of one of the animals and pretend that it is now a couple of days into the journey. Talk directly to your audience for three or four minutes, telling them enough about your background and the problems you face in order to make them want to read the entire book.

4. Pantomime the meal the old man "shared" with the animals. (Afterward, you might write interior monologues that reveal the thoughts the man and each animal were having.)

5. Discuss *The Incredible Journey* with students who have read other survival stories, such as *Julie of the Wolves* or *Call it Courage*. One student acts as scribe and records interesting insights, patterns noted, etc. for later sharing with the whole group.

Writing
1. Write chapter titles.

2. Write a diamente poem that compares the trio at the begininning of their journey, and at the end. A diamente is a diamond-shaped poem of 7 lines:
    Line 1: one noun subject
    Line 2: two adjectives
    Line 3: three participles
    Line 4: four nouns related to the subject
    Line 5: three participles
    Line 6: two adjectives
    Line 7: one noun, opposite of subject.
(Feel free to vary the format, i.e. 2,4,6,8,6,4,2, or use different parts of speech.)

3. List as many character/personality traits as you can for each of the animals.

4. Create a timeline that shows when key events in the story happened in relation to each other (Day 1, Day 2, etc.)

5. Suppose John had written to "Dear Gabby" for advice about what to do when he found out that his three "charges" were missing. Write his letter and the letter of advice that he receives.

6. Suppose a local reporter had decided to write a "human interest" story about the Hunters, their pets, and their pets' journey. Write the report, complete with quotes from interviews you had with different people who saw the pets at various points in their journey.

7. Write a paragraph explaining what the poem by Whitman (that precedes the story) has to do with the story.

8. Write an essay defending or refuting the following statement, made by critic Fran Ashdown: "All of the animals...are invested with commendable traits and human-like emotions. Burnford created a memorable story but not one that is a fair representation of the true nature of animals."

9. When Longridge was on the phone, the Terrier used the opportunity to "get away with something." Write a paragraph describing a time this reminds you of when a pet or child exploited a situation (used it to get away with something).

10. Helvi helps nurse the cat back to health. Describe a time when you helped nurse a sick or injured animal. Be sure to include facts about what you did as well as feelings, "low" points as well as "high" ones.

11. Write a paragraph comparing how the dogs and cat greet each other with how people greet each other after absences.

12. Chart the setting, characters, episodes, and resolution of the story on a story map.

13. Using *The Incredible Journey* as a model, write your own animal survival tale.

Language Study

1. Make a list of the words that are used to describe the personality of each animal.

2. Burnford uses many vivid action words. Make a list of your favorite verbs, found in the novel.

3. Make a list of expressions used in the book, such as "beyond the pale." Try to find out how the expressions originated.

Art

1. Analyze the illustrations done by Carl Burger. How did he make them? Why are/aren't they effective? Would you prefer color?

2. Create a filmstrip retelling of the story by drawing about 20 key scenes on acetate and recording the accompanying narration.

3. Create a shoebox diorama that shows a key scene from the story, such as the animals' visit to the old man's cabin. (Use clay, styrofoam, small plastic figures, magazine cut-outs, etc.)

4. As a group project, create a picture chart that identifies the various plants and animals mentioned in the story (e.g., Siamese cat, Labrador Retriever, Bull Terrier, lynx, asters, fisher, etc.) and tells a bit about each.

5. In a small group, create a "mobile map" of the story to remind you of the important parts of the story as you retell it. Attach poster board cut-outs to the mobile, labeled, "character," "setting" and "plot." (Each labeled cut-out should show something from the story, such as characters—the three pets, setting—the Ojibway campfire, plot—the fight between the lynx and the cat, etc.) From each of the labels, attach strips of paper describing the particular characters, particular settings, and words or phrases that summarize steps in the plot.

Music

1. As a group project, collect recordings of music you would use in the background if you were filming the movie.

2. Pretend this novel has been made into a TV series and you have been hired to write the song that opens each show. Write the lyrics for a song about the adventures of the three pets. Set the lyrics to a well-known tune or write one of your own.

Geography/Math

Map the journey taken by the three pets. Calculate the distances (in kilometers, as used in Canada) between landmarks.

Research

1. Study the behavior of cats and dogs. Create a "Fact or Fiction?" book. On one page write the phrase "True or False?" followed by a statement about cats or dogs (e.g. "True or False?—Cats are more intelligent than dogs." On the next page tell whether the statement is true or false and why.

2. Clip articles out of magazines and newspapers that remind you of the story in some way because they tell about similar events, problems, animals, etc. Create bulletin boards by labeling each article with a caption that explains the similarity to *The Incredible Journey*.

Cooperative Groups as a Strategy with the Novel Units Approach

Many teachers find that student cooperative work groups serve multiple purposes. These groups provide a forum for students to process information, as well as a means for students to practice interpersonal skills. Many researcher/educators find that the most successful cooperative learning efforts feature group goals (cooperative groups working together to complete a project, achieve group recognition, etc.), but have individual accountability (group success depending on the individual learning of all group members). *Novel Units* are ideal for use by cooperative groups. Following are two of the numerous ways the guides might be used to promote cooperative learning.

Approach #1

Divide the class into groups of four to focus on the novel. Assign the following jobs (explained below) to various group members: **Literary Enhancer, Discussion Director, Vocabulary Enricher,** and **Group Recorder.** If cooperative learning is a new strategy, the teacher initially discusses appropriate group behaviors including: keeping voices down, how to voice criticism of others' ideas in a supportive way, how group participation will translate into an individual final evaluation.

Then the teacher either models each of the *Novel Unit* jobs listed above using a short literature selection or uses four learning stations in which all literary enhancers meet together, all discussion directors convene, etc. The teacher (and others such as parent volunteers, aides, or students who have had experience with the approach) assists at various stations. Students are rotated through all stations so that they will be familiar with all jobs.

If the entire class is reading the same novel, the teacher assigns the section (chapter, scene, or pages) for the day. Part of the class period might be devoted to whole group discussion or activities (outlined in the *Novel Units Teacher's Guide*). During the remainder of the period, the class might be broken into cooperative groups. (These groups might discuss the same questions, or they might discuss different questions and report back to the whole group later with a summary of their discussion.)

If students are reading different novels, the teacher assigns the section to be covered by each group. Individual students complete their particular tasks (below) for sharing with the cooperative group after reading the assigned section.

Literary Enhancer: The Literary Enhancer might lead a discussion of various responses to student activity sheets from the *Novel Units Student Packet* that focus on literary analysis: attribute webs, story maps, etc. Alternatively, the literary enhancer might choose 3-5 passages for discussion and/or oral reading. Passages might be chosen because they contain:
- (1) interesting dialogue
- (2) appealing description
- (3) exciting, funny, crucial parts
- (4) examples of the author's setting a mood
- (5) examples of particular literary techniques such as flashback or foreshadowing.

Vocabulary Enricher: The Vocabulary Enricher might be responsible for providing answers to vocabulary activity sheets found in the student packet and leading a discussion of these answers. Alternatively, the vocabulary enricher might choose 4-7 vocabulary words from the novel or play to present to the group. Good word choices could be:
- (1) unfamiliar words with good context clues
- (2) unfamiliar words to look up in the dictionary
- (3) words used in a unique way
- (4) foreign words, technical words, or words that are hard to pronounce.

The job includes planning how to introduce the words to the group.

Discussion/Comprehension Director: This person's task varies with the piece of literature under study. Roles include:
- (1) calling the group to order
- (2) reading aloud discussion questions (contained in the Teacher's Guide)
- (3) acknowledging discussants who are ready to share ideas
- (4) guiding the discussion so that most of the questions are considered during the time period allotted for discussion.

Alternatively, the discussion director might prepare 5-8 questions about the assigned pages.

Group Recorder: This person fills in the group recorder sheet, collects the assignments, announces jobs for the next session, and turns in the papers to the teacher.

See pages 31 and 32 for forms that can be used for all of these Novel Unit jobs.

Approach #2

When the whole class is studying the same piece of literature, students can be assigned to groups of two or three. During class time, the teacher directs instruction for about half the time, using the *Novel Units Teacher's Guide* for discussion and activities. Then students divide into their pairs or triads to complete various activities, including (1) partner reading, (2) story-related writing, (3) vocabulary activities, and (4) story retelling. When students have completed these activities, their partners initial a student assignment form indicating that they have completed their tasks. A sample student assignment form is shown on the next page.

Name: _____ **Date:** _____

For this reading assignment, our group, including:

_____   _____

_____   _____

completed the following activities:

_____

_____

_____

This went well:

_____

_____

We need to work on: _____

_____

We need help with: _____

_____

Signed,

_____   _____

_____   _____

Reading Assignment: _____ **Name:** _____ **Date:** _____

LITERARY ENHANCER: Guides discussion of author's technique/purpose.

Section	Reason (1-5)	Plan for Sharing/Reading

Choices could include:
1. Good dialogue between characters
2. Vivid description
3. Setting a mood
4. Example of author's craft: (a) simile/metaphor; (b) foreshadowing, (c) flashback
5. Other: _____

Reading Assignment: _____ **Name:** _____ **Date:** _____

VOCABULARY ENRICHER: Clarifies word meanings and pronunciations.

Page	Word	Description	Plan

Presentation plan possibilities:
1. Have group find the word and use context clues.
2. Use dictionary. Choose the correct meaning.
3. Use thesaurus. Substitute a synonym in the story.
4. Create analogies using the word.
5. Other: _____

© Novel Units, Inc.   All rights reserved

Reading Assignment: _____

Name: _____ **Date:** _____

DISCUSSION DIRECTOR: Asks comprehension and higher level discussion questions; leads discussion.

Prompts:
Summarize _____
What do you think _____?
How is _____ like/different from _____?
How did you feel about _____?
What happened after _____?
What do you think caused _____?
Why did _____?
What might have happened if _____?
If the author had left out _____, how would the story have been changed?

On the back of this sheet, summarize group predictions about the WHO, WHAT, and WHERE of the next section of the story.

Reading Assignment: _____

Name: _____ **Date:** _____

GROUP RECORDER: Evaluates and records group members' participation and performance.

Name	Job	Done	Participation/ Cooperation	Read

Participation/Cooperation:
  X Satisfactory
  + Extra contribution/cooperation
  - Distracting/Interrupting

© Novel Units, Inc.   All rights reserved

Essay Evaluation Form

1. **Focus:** Student writes a clear thesis
   and includes it in the opening paragraph.   10   8   4

2. **Organization:** The final draft reflects
   the assigned outline; transitions are
   used to link ideas.   20   16   12

3. **Support:** Adequate details are provided;
   extraneous details are omitted.   12   10   7

4. **Detail:** Each quote or reference is explained
   (as if the teacher had not read the book);
   ideas are not redundant.   12   10   7

5. **Mechanics:** Spelling, capitalization, and
   usage are correct.   16   12   8

6. **Sentence Structure:** The student avoids
   run-ons and sentence fragments.   10   8   4

7. **Verb:** All verbs are in the correct tense;
   sections in which plot is summarized are
   in the present tense.   10   8   4

8. **Total effect of the essay.**   10   8   4

                                                100   80   50

Comments:

                                          Total: _____

(This rubric may be altered to fit the needs of a particular class. You may wish to show it to students before they write their essays. They can use it as a self-evaluation tool, and they will be aware of exactly how their essays will be graded.)

Evaluation: Alternative Means of Assessment

While the tests included in the Student Packet for this *Novel Unit* are useful vehicles for evaluation, the most productive types of evaluation may well involve no grades at all.

For example, discussion is an essential ingredient in the *Novel Units* approach. One way to involve students in self-evaluation is to videotape some literature discussion groups. An evaluation sheet can be devised through joint effort of teacher and students and used by students as they watch themselves on tape. (Sample items: "I sometimes relate my ideas to what others in the group have offered." "I am sometimes willing to risk disagreeing with others.")

In addition, students can be encouraged to reflect on their participation in discussion groups (and potential areas for improvement) through ongoing journal entries.

The portfolio approach is becoming widely accepted; many teachers encourage students to participate in the selection of representative samples of materials to be kept in one file. Such materials might include: completed activity sheets from the Student Packet, extension activities, writing samples, response logs, and lists of titles read in literature groups or in addition to class work. These folders can be used in conjunction with more traditional evaluation instruments (i.e., graded tests) as a basis for assigning term grades, a measurement of growth to share with parents during parent-teacher conferences, and—perhaps most important—evidence of growth for students themselves.

Notes

Notes